MW01047206

The Touchstone

ROBYN SARAH

The Touchstone

POEMS NEW & SELECTED

First published in 1992 by
House of Anansi Press Limited
1800 Steeles Avenue West
Concord, Ontario
L4K 2P3

Canadian Cataloguing in Publication Data

Sarah, Robyn, 1949-
  The touchstone

ISBN 0-88784-528-2

I. Title.

PS8587.A7T6 1992   C811'.54   C92-093376-9
PR9199.3.S3T6 1992

Typesetting: Tony Gordon Ltd.

Printed and bound in Canada

The author wishes to acknowledge the support of the
Canada Council.

House of Anansi Press gratefully acknowledges the support
of the Canada Council, Ontario Arts Council and Ontario
Publishing Centre in the development of writing and
publishing in Canada.

*To the memory
of my grandmother*

*Adela Hirschhorn Palker
1900 - 1990*

Contents

SELECTED POEMS 1970 – 1986

New Poems

1986 – 1990

Journey

In this house, the furnace and the furnace-pump
make a rumble that shivers the panes
and rattles the rads, till the whole room
throbs like an oiltruck, idling.

And when they shut off: what silence!
In the window, hung by a thread,
a teardrop prism emits a purple spark.
Beneath it, a crocheted snowflake

revolves slowly, seeming to melt into air
at ninety degrees, and then to reappear.
Only a little sun
ever gets in. It's here now —

Then the heat starts up again. Slowly
the rumble picks up a rhythm, something like
the rackety rocking of a train. I close my eyes
and let it carry me . . .

I will remember this house
for its thundering winters, for the
huge distances they
carried me.

Passages

All day long, upstairs,
a new mother coos to her baby girl,
and the floorboards creak, creak
under her rocking-chair.

And footsteps go back and forth,
back and forth, in the dead of night,
and yellow light from her kitchen window
suddenly floods the snow.

Coo, coo; motherhood has turned her
into a bird. Silently I tell her: I, too,
once woke in the night with hardened breasts,
and soaked the front of my flannel gown with milk.

Now my daughter stands splay-legged at the mirror
braiding her hair against night-time tangles,
and already her nipples have begun to stand out,
and she crosses her arms over them, shyly.

And upstairs, you read books about infant growth,
with pages of gleaming photographs —
and downstairs, I read books about divorce,
with no photographs at all.

And all day long, snow blows in small showers
from the tree whose branches brush your window.
Bursts of bright powder, glittery in the sun,
fall past my window.

A Night Window

Looking at losing you;
it's far away,
like headlights
that haven't yet crested the hill,
just a weird glow
in the sky —

or it's very near,
something to get
excited about, like
glimpsing what turns out to be
my eyelash, brushing
the microscope lens —

Looking at it like
looking at my
own face the dark pane
gives back: at what it sees,
neither surprised
nor resigned.

A Mystery

Around the side of Bob
Jones' barn the children find
the dead calf, frozen
among dry weeds and
scrap wood, small icicles
in his shag, ice
on his muzzle. He is like
a carved calf, dropped in the snow
as if in his very tracks,
his front feet bent
as though in mid-trot, his
flank emaciated, bony structure
looming. A sculpture of a
white calf, lying on its side
in the snow at the side
of the barn, among things
cast off and forgotten.

Around his neck the rope
halter still dangles, beaded
with ice. They stop
a few feet away, silent, and stand
gravely looking, framing the thought
'Is it real?' — Not 'Is it alive,'
for they know at once it is
not that. But is it real
and not a toy, is a thing still real

once dead, a calf like a
plaster calf, lying frozen
in the snow, cast off
in its perfect stillness,
laid aside even though
perfect, looking realer
than real, untouchable, utterly
other?

The Touchstone

Let it rest, then, shall we?
(And what will break
the back of this winter — cold
into equinox, still no give
to the branches, no play?)
A lovely love
is ending. Then,
let it rest . . .

Old Madame Dubé in the
next bed, the one
who doesn't know what's what,
she thinks she knows me,
holds out her hands to me, each time,
tries to catch hold. I hear her
behind the curtain, at night,
crying. Her people
are good, though, they come,
the priest comes;
some of them, here, their
people don't come, no one comes.

We had a lot of
good weeks, many good weeks.
It was sunny a lot, we
can't complain. They said just
leave the key on the sill

by the front door, leave everything
as you found it. And don't forget
to switch the power off
when you go.

Suddenly the trees have been bare
for a long time. My
alligator hands, my turtle claws;
winter that raises nails
from the dry floorboards, sparks
from the hair —
Where were you, yesterday? I had
this thought, on the bus,
coming home: that love
is a touchstone,
that we must make it one
in our lives, to live well.
(Then it seemed
I was asleep. I woke up
past my stop.)

Simply to begin again, in the rain,
in the unexpected air, mild,
spring-scented, when will that come?
I want to open my coat, get wet, it's time
for me to take my name off the list
and start walking.

Sometimes a man

Sometimes a man who has missed his bus
still runs after it a little way.
You can see his shoulders first
subside, defeated, but he doesn't slow;
his head knows that it's too late,
but his feet have to go on a bit
doing what they were doing . . . so.
That's how it is, with feet.

The Thinkers

After the thaw, slickfreeze.
Out of the subway
morning throngs
move tight-shouldered
across an icefield

And if any relax his guard
even a second, to admit
a thought's free movement,
he feels his feet
slide out from under him —

Nor need look far
to find one similarly struck,
as every here and there, another
is seen to stagger
and recover or
go down.

Shell

I have your hat
in my hands; hat
that holds your head,
what does it know?
And were I to halloo
down into it, to yell
Hey! who lives here?
what could it tell me
of the head it holds?
That old cold head
that won't disclose
its holdings . . . Love,
I have your hat; keep
what I say under it,
along with what
you don't. (Hat
that holds your head
I would hold
in my hands
instead.)

Caught

What decides a squirrel
to move?
A cold squirrel,
upright on a post,
tail raised and flattened
against his back
as a man turns his collar up
for shelter   And wind
tousling the hairs of it,
wind with a bite.

How quietly he sits
on groomed haunches,
not eating or looking
at a thing. But cold.
The hard earth
is frozen now   And wind
rattles the brown leaves —

Till suddenly he turns
and on what whim runs
rippling to ground?
Hungry, or wanting
a change of position,
or merely spooked —
A cold squirrel I see today
caught in his own life,
seeming
his own mover.

Letter

When you come back, this time,
will you take me to you
as something that has been lost and
found again — gratefully, gladly;
will you drink me on one breath,
like one who has run miles?
Or will it be otherwise;
will you be a little
shy and stiff, like a child
with a foreign aunt; or worse,
will you pretend it has not
been with us, as it has been?

During your absence the leaves
have been opening, the small
tight buds of lily-of-the-valley
push from their sheath.
But still there is that
Japanese spacing, where each small leaf
shows clear against the sky
and one can see the bough
between them, the whole
branch-structure, logic
of trees . . .

When you come back, it will
be past, this time of clarity;
you will come straight to a
fullness of leaves, drinking the light
at windows, a green
deep as forgetting.

I think of this daily.
There are things I should not
be worrying about, now,
if I knew you less well,
or if I knew you better.

Once, Desire

Once, desire was a soft roaring
between us, like white water,
and we adjusted our voices
to be heard above it
till it seemed to us
that we whispered: as any sound,
heard long enough, becomes silence.

I would like to go back to that time,
when the power was still outside of us
and we were as if asleep, cocooned
in the white rush of it. Unharmed
and unarmed. When we were a
dream of wings. Before this
perilous flying.

Without You

Without you
I am calm,
but it is the calm of a small boat
that goes nowhere, a boat
lying flat on the water.
Look, the little boat that needs
no rope to hold it!
It will not go anywhere,
but sits in one place
not even rocking.

I am calm, but
it is the calm
of a kite on the ground.
Nothing will persuade it
to ride upward
and shiver its ribbons
in the sunlight,
And a kite without wind,
what is that?

Without you I am calm.
Yes:
dead-calm.

But I want to be alive!
But I want to travel!

Residue

The iron aftertaste
of too much tea
on the tongue —
Days lost to love —
that, love once lost, remain
like motes to ride
the waters of the eye —
Sand in a shoe, miles
from the sandy shore:
sad residue —
these grains spilled out
on the tired grain
of floor.

Four Farmers

I said (looking at the tidy rows of his planted garden):
you know, I can't do it like that, I can't plot it all out in
advance and plant logically, a garden is so abstract to me
until I see it growing. I can only plant on impulse, by blind
whim, at the moment and on the spot. I don't even leave
markers . . .

And he said: that doesn't matter, there's a book I read by
a Japanese gardener who doesn't make rows at all, he
doesn't break the earth, he just takes the seed in hand-
fuls, all mixed up, and scatters it here and there on the
ground.

Now, while we were talking, a gust of wind rushed up the
valley and picked up the opened seed-packets his small
son had left lying on the wooden deck. And while we were
talking, the wind was planting a Japanese garden all
around us in the uncut grass.

Mutual

The window is what the flowers need:
the flowers are what the window needs.

A woman
feels this, does not
know it, places the flowers
there, so. Raises
the sash.

But it asks a man
to see it.

Trial Footage: The Farm

It begins with a man standing alone in the middle of his field, looking at nothing;

It begins with the standing bones of a dead elm, standing elm bones;

With a child on a fence, looking up at clouds moving past the dead elm, and feeling how the tree is slowly falling . . .

Or with a child lying in the grass, looking up at clouds moving past the barn roof, and feeling how the barn is slowly falling . . .

Or with the same child, thinking that he is feeling the earth turn.

It begins with a man standing alone in the middle of his barn, looking at nothing;

It begins with a car taking a curve on a dirt road and sliding off the shoulder into the ditch, slow motion, and coming to rest at a sharp angle against a wall of brush,

And in the silence a child in the back seat cries out, "I'm scared — we're going to die!" though the car has already stopped moving.

It begins with a man far down in the lower pasture, his blue shirt glimpsed between trees,

Or with a woman's call to supper, moments before sunset, answered by silence and a rush of wind.

It begins with the child finding an empty bullet case in the dust by the side of the road, and slipping it into his pocket,

Or finding a dead mole by the side of the road, and stroking its velvet fur, and marveling at its human hands, and digging a hole to bury it beside the barn.

It begins with a man standing alone on a plowed field, looking at nothing,

And it begins to rain on his bare neck, on the slope of his shoulders,

And it begins to wet the lightened hairs on his strong arms hanging loose at his sides,

And it rains down harder on his head, that he lowers against the rain,

It rains on his unruly head.

A man has to make waves

A man has to make
waves, somehow, or he's not happy.
A woman, children, can't
make him happy — only warm him —
only give him an ear
to air his yearnings, his yen to make waves.

What is it, in a man?
It is an unquiet thing in him,
a thing that beats
like a ram in a thicket,
 — nor will be still
until he seize it by the horns
and offer it up to God.

The Trust

Once I dreamed that a dead friend
wrote me a letter from beyond, complete
with return address; when I awoke
the name of the street eluded me,
but I remembered the message, a
short one, only this,
he wanted to tell me:
"The work goes on."

And when my grandfather lay
in the hospital, settling his account
with cancer, he replied
to all who inquired, "I'm just
waiting for a visa," he would say.
"Tell them, I'm waiting for a visa."

And I remember
how he looked at me, two days
before the end —
looked and looked,
as if to store me up —
and held me with his eyes
intent in love; and then
how he closed them, saying
"I can still see you, I see you
with my eyes closed. I'll
remember you." Smiling.

A good death, it's a gift
to the living. To be remembered
when we're gone, to remember our dead, these
we know are to be desired. But to be
remembered by our dead!   that
is something else — a trust,
a blessing.

Equinox

All the gold has drained
from the light; and these leaves,
littering the grass, caught
in its tangles, where
did they come from?

There was a black horse, one evening,
across a fence, who followed us
a length of the road —

I must have been asleep
all summer.

Terminal

Summer's last puff

coming in over the brownlands
like an embalming,

the way a plowed field fills
suddenly with gulls
blinding white
in November's sun;

a dream-wind,
carrying the ghost of greenness
from far away —

and from far away too
this sun that skirts
the girders, going
no higher,

a squinting sun,
touching with lukewarm
fingers the
crumpled heads
of the marigolds

Flower

The small flower of another, this
is what we had, and held,
and did not take for granted — , no — ,
it was so like the underwings
of moths that fold away
their colours —
                          These
are the brown days again,
the shut fan; who can say
how many times an old stem
has in it left to blossom?
Wait with me —

November of the long echo.
Whispers in standing straw.

Ad Lib for Bone Flute

The news today is better
than the news yesterday,
but the news today
is not good.
Yesterday I saw they had chopped down
the old maple tree.
Today
it's still gone.

Remembering, *remembrance*:
a lilac-smelling word,
a word like a papered room
at the top of some stairs, the
windows thrown open, sunlight
coming in with cool air
and a breath of lilac.
The wallpaper is important,
and the sunlight, glancing suddenly
off a mirror.
Outside this room
somebody has waxed the wooden bannister
and is polishing it with a flannel cloth.

These are the last days
of sun on these
particular walls.
Accept my story:
there was a time
when it all made sense,

coffee and chocolate rolls
on the porch, Sunday mornings,
and the garden, the little garden,
our pride, twinkling
in the sun —
and earlier, years earlier,
snow mornings in rented rooms,
Dufay on the stereo, the cat
walking on the breakfast table;
I do not remember any more
the cups we then drank from,
or the copper kettle, that like a ship
sunk on its maiden voyage, lasted
only a day.
But I remember that your foot bled
when you crushed the wineglass
and we did not even think
to think it ominous,
and I remember a terrible silence
that it snowed into, every winter,
and the dry pinecones in a basket
in the window-bay, popping their seeds
in the dead of night.

Once on a rainy lake
in the foggy first light,
you blew long flute notes
across a tent pole,

a hollow cylinder, aluminum,
held upright; so what had
sustained a roof above us
the night before, became
a lonely music, breathed out
across the water

And the small flames licked up
where you coaxed them, hunched
in the drizzle, blowing on live coals
from the banked fire,
and we drank our coffee
out of tin cups, murky
and tasting of cinders, and were glad.

But that was a moment
of breaking surface,
like the loons we watched that morning,
coming up each time a little
farther off, till our eyes ached
with looking; and there were
other moments, too many of them,
of a different tenor;
of hard, bright, dry-eyed wakefulness
running on into pre-dawn,
and the grey light at the frozen windows,

and old pipes coming to life
with a cold clanking, a sound
like chains.

This is not what
I asked for, though I can trace
its onset, back to our earliest
closet kitchens.
You knew we would not
grow old together.

The tent of family has collapsed,
has slipped its pinnings,
leaving us whistling in the rain.
But of the strong cloth, now,
let us make coverings,
and let us of the rib
make music.

The Strength

Doomed beauty: daisies
before snow.
Old neighbourhoods.
The woodlot. Our
house of cards.

What but your love
remembered, could give me
the strength
to turn a sunny face
to you now?

Radical

Cutting down the ivy

like cutting the hair
a woman has been wont
to hide behind:

luxuriant tumbles
the weight of it
to ground

lies
heaped there —

sun
on the bark again,
air
at the nape

Nisi

In defence of each other we
said goodbye, shook hands.
In defence of ourselves
we moved on, ships
of our own names,
churning the water behind us
in separate wakes. Simple.
We parted company. Became
two, as we had been
before. A commonplace;
an alteration to the résumé,
a new tax status. Simple.
Everybody knows about this.
No one
cares to know more.

How does one think about those years?
A weight of sadness, like the weight
of snow on a roof. It is not
substantial, as snow is
"only water," but the weight of it
is enough to bow the roof in, you
can't discount it.

And the documents, out of which
every breathing thing has been edited —
not a hair, not a shred
of pipe tobacco, blanket fluff,
orange peel, no, not a

shirt button or a bobby pin,
but tidied — pulled tight — blocked clean
as a hospital bed —
how does one read them?
One does not read them. One
files them.

There is a lot of paper
left over, most of it
of limited interest. There are
the photographs, warped records, the dated
inscriptions in books, many
frayed drawings with old scotch tape
darkening at the corners, the pill vial
half full of baby teeth.
There is the basement, where, without warning,
one can be struck dumb, stabbed to the heart,
by a broken toy. None of this is
really interesting. Not to speak of,
or to be spoken of.
Not to write home about.

It ends like this, one walks
out of the dark courthouse
into the sun. From here on there is
one thing in your life that
no one can know the like of
but you.

Burning the Journals

The past is useless
to me now:
an old suitcase
with mould in the lining,
heavy even when empty —

heavy empty,
like the bronze bell
of the Russian church,
clapperless
in the grass;

so I shall have to go
on from here with less
to bank on. My peeled eye.
The way things sing
in the sun.

Selected Poems

1970 – 1986

Sinkers

If in sudden and several places the ground
you walked on wore thin, or opened up
clear through to the other side — what then?
I can remember when it did: spring rain
left holes in parking lots — holes full of sky
where clouds bloomed and expanded like the milk in tea.
We liked to stand on the edge of them: look down
at what we knew was up, but might as well
exist below as above us (why not?) — and tease ourselves
with fear of falling in. Of stepping
one step too far, right over the edge and
down, down into sky without end. Only, to try
with just one round-toed rubber boot, was to bend
the window back into water: once wavy,
that sky lost its power to pull us in.

Now rain-pools are just things to walk around
or step over. But to keep the ground
from seeming too sure under us, there are eyes
that open up bottomless as those sky-holes
to catch us in our tracks. And we keep dreaming
of a clean fall through to the other side —
unasked-for, with a cushioned landing
and no charge for the ride.

Broom at Twilight

Some climbs end nowhere. Like the unplanned climb
I took this evening.
                              I'd gone down the beach
some little way, and though the sun was low,
I thought that it would see me round those rocks
to the next cove, with time enough to watch
the tide come in (and maybe make it back
without getting my feet wet.)
                              No such luck —
beyond that stretch, the tide was in already,
and there was nothing to do but climb the cliffs
up to the road, and walk back home that way.

Dark doesn't wait, this time of year. I climbed,
and the sun went down as I went up. Went right on
falling beyond the unseen edge faster
than I could find my holds. (Footholds in clay,
handholds on anchored roots. And all the while
the sky fast darkening out from above.)
                              Near water,
the grey hour's luminous. And by the beach
I should have had no trouble finding my way.
Where I came up, though — something blocked the light.
It was the sameness that surprised me.
                              Broom:

a forest of it. Higher than my head.
And not in clumps, the way it seems to grow
by day — but in a solid wall. An army
bristling with strange intent. The broom I knew
grew in tall waving tufts like uncut hay
to wade through at high noon. This broom stood up
like earth's raised hackles in the failing light —
a massing of ominous spikes against the sky
and stems that wouldn't give way. I couldn't find
the mouse-paths children make to get to the sea —
but had to plunge (broom closing over me)
into a tangible edgeless element,
banking on where I thought the road must be.

October / Sutton

We climbed the pasture hill to haul down wood
from the damp pile beside the sugar-shack:
five of us, single file on the stone wall
to keep our feet out of the marsh — Once there,
you stacked the rounds to fill each helper's arms,
and you and I were the last back.

You gave me almost more than I could hold —
a great weight of dark damp logs, the smell of the bark
coming loose, leaving marks on my bare arms.
When I was halfway down the hill
I knew without looking, you were up there still,
standing a little bemused in the sunlit clearing,
maybe listening, maybe only half hearing
a loud jay on the sugar-shack roof . . .

Things I had wanted to say, but there seemed no words
so we exchanged silences, and that was good.
 — You loaded my arms with logs, I brought them down
and set them in your shed — and that said it all
for both of us. Whether or not you understood,
it was a kind of gift — that wood.

I think of your hands

I think of your hands
in midwinter. Of a darkness they pulled over me
in last summer's grass, under dying
stars. And their stillness, later,
upturned at your sides, touched
by the chill of dew, before you sat up
to cup them round a match-flame
in the damp of morning.
                        All these months of cold,
(dew on the window splintering
into shapes of grass and stars)
the thought, like a spilled coal,
has been burning a slow hole
in the nap of winter.

He hears her on the stairs

He hears her on the stairs, but for the moment
the page holds him.
There will be time enough to mark the place,
lay down the book, and cross the lighted hall
to let her in . . .

— But she,
watching him through the glass that separates
night and the rain from the dry room beyond
and hand from hand,
remembers who he is, knows what she knows
and knows this pane to be a precious thing.

Touch knuckles to this were sacrilege!
and so she stands, her face
pressed on the dark glass
like a leaf under ice.

Paperweight

i

She accustoms herself
to his silences. They seem
rich, like soup; slow, like
soup. They heat up slowly
and thicken. There is no
telling what is in them.

ii

He moves the furniture around.
He reads cookbooks.

iii

She dreams she has broken
his little hammer, the one he uses
to play tunes on the base of his lamp.
(He has no little hammer.)

iv

He picks up the papers
wind has scattered from her desk.
He gives her an old candle
for a paperweight. (In a note

he tells her to use it
as a paperweight.)

v

When he isn't there
she notices things
that trouble her. When he
is there, she notices
the same things.

vi

He wakes up at night
and thinks he hears pages
turning.

Fugue

Women are on their way
to the new country. The men watch
from high office windows
while the women go.
They do not get very far
in a day. You can still see them
from high office windows.

Women are on their way
to the new country. They are taking
it all with them: rugs,
pianos, children. Or they are leaving
it all behind them: cats,
plants, children.
They do not get very far in a day.

Some women travel alone
to the new country. Some
with a child, or children.
Some go in pairs or groups
or in pairs with a child
or children. Some in a group with
cats, plants, children.

They do not get very far in a day.
They must stop to bake bread on the road
to the new country, and to share

bread with other women. Children
outgrow their clothes and shed them
for smaller children. The women too
shed clothes, put on each other's

cats, plants, children, and at full moon
no one remembers the way to the new country
where there will be room for everyone and
it will be summer and children will
shed their clothes and the loaves will
rise without yeast and women will have come
so far that no one can see them, even from

high office windows.

Maintenance

Sometimes the best I can do
is homemade soup, or a patch on the knee
of the baby's overalls.
Things you couldn't call poems.
Things that spread in the head,
that swallow
whole afternoons, weigh down the week
till the elastic's gone right out of it —
so gone
it doesn't even snap when it breaks.
And one spent week's
just like the shapeless bag
of another. Monthsful of them,
with new ones rolling in and
filling up with the same junk: toys
under the bed, eggplant slices sweating
on the breadboard, the washing machine
spewing suds into the toilet, socks
drying on the radiator and falling down
behind it where the dust lies furry and
full of itself . . . The dust!
what I could tell you about
the dust. How it eats things —
pencils, caps from ballpoint pens,
plastic sheep, alphabet blocks.
How it spins cocoons
around them, clumps up and
smothers whatever strays into
its reaches — buttons,

pennies, marbles — and then
how it lifts all-of-a-piece,
dust-pelts
thick as the best velvet
on the bottom of the mop.
                              Sometimes
the best that I can do
is maintenance: the eaten
replaced by the soon-to-be-eaten, the raw
by the cooked, the spilled-on
by the washed and dried, the ripped
by the mended; empty cartons
heaved down the cellar stairs, the
cans stacked on the ledge, debris
sealed up in monstrous snot-green bags
for the garbage man.

And I'll tell you what
they don't usually tell you: there's no
poetry in it. There's no poetry
in scraping concrete off the high-chair tray
with a bent kitchen knife, or fishing
with broomstick behind the fridge
for a lodged ball. None in the sink
that's always full, concealing its cargo
of crockery under a head
of greasy suds. Maybe you've heard

that there are compensations? That, too's
a myth. It doesn't work that way.
The planes are separate. Even if there are
moments each day that take you by the heart
and shake the dance back into it, that you lost
the beat of, somewhere years behind — even if
in the clear eye of such a moment you catch
a glimpse of the only thing worth looking for —
to call this compensation, is to demean.
The planes are separate. And it's the
other one, the one called maintenance,
I mostly am shouting about.
I mean the day-to-day,
that bogs the mind, voice, hands
with things you couldn't call poems.
I mean the thread that breaks.
The dust between
typewriter keys.

Pardon Me

The rip in the sleeve of your jacket, and the fact that I do not have to mend it, are conjoined in a way that you do not understand. You do not understand because you do not know that there is a rip in the sleeve of your jacket, and I do not have to tell you because I do not have to mend it. This is not the same as to say that I do not have to mend it because I am not going to tell you it is there, which would be a stall at best. Maybe you do know that there is a rip in the sleeve of your jacket, but if you do, you would not mention it to me because you know that I do not have to mend it.

Because I do not have to mend it, and because you do not seem to mind wearing it with a rip in the sleeve, your jacket is becoming a kind of statement to me of all that does and does not exist between us, including what you do not know about what I feel about your wearing it with a rip in the sleeve. There is also what I do not know about what you would feel if you knew my feelings. I am not going to tell you what I feel about your wearing your jacket with a rip in the sleeve because if you do not know there is a rip in the sleeve, you might be less than pleased to find out — especially as I do not have to mend it. Moreover, I might be less than pleased to find out that had you known there was a rip in the sleeve, you would not have been wearing your jacket.

To avoid mutual disappointment, I do not touch on this matter which, even assuming you do know there is a rip in the sleeve, you are doubtless not thinking about. Besides, there is always the danger that my mention of a rip in the sleeve might be interpreted as an offer to mend it, a desire to mend it, or a wish to see it mended. That is not what I meant at all; that is not it, at all.

Woman on a Bus

The hat that is out
of the ordinary, the off-beat
hat, lends to the face
that is ordinary, an odd
off-beat grace. (It's all in how
she carries herself, that she
carries it off.)

Cat's Cradle

When women together sit sipping
cold tea and tugging at the
threads of memory, thoughtfully
pulling at this
or that bit or loop, or slipping
this loop over that finger till
warp and weft of past lives begin
crazily to unwind, when women sit
smoking and talking, the talk
making smoke in the air, when they shake
shreds of tobacco out of a crumpled pack
and keep drinking the same weak tea
from the same broken pot, something clicks
in the springs of the clock
and it's yesterday again,
and the sprung yarn rolls down loose
from the spool of the moon.

When women together sit talking
an afternoon, when they talk
the sun down, talk stars, talk
dawn — they talk up a dust
of sleeping dogs and bones
and they talk a drum for the dust
to dance to, till the dance
drums up a storm; when women
sit drumming fingers on tops
of tables, when the tables turn
into tops that spin and hum

and the bobbin of the moon
keeps spinning its fine yarn down
to catch fingers, when fingers catch
talk in a cat's cradle, and turn
talk into a net to catch the curve
of the storm — then it's talk
against talk, till the tail
of the storm trails into dust
and they talk the dust back down.

Things that matter and don't matter
are caught together, things done and undone,
and the kettle boils dry and over
while they lean closer to peer down
into the murky water where last night's dream
flicks its tail and is gone
(and the reel of the moon keeps cranking
its long line down) — when women together
sit sipping cold tea and sawing on the strings
of memory, it is an old tune.
The rice sticks to the bottom of the pan,
and things get left out in the rain.

End to End

Feet, how did you get so far away?
I watch you from the other end
of the bathtub — the pair of you,
animals, carrying me around
thirty years now, like good
beasts of burden. Time was
when I saddled you first in
patent leather, you dazzled
my eyes, showing me my
face, twinned, in black lacquer.
Then you were nearer; near
the years I rode you hard
in scuffed Oxfords, rode you
bare, summers, over
beach-shingle, road-gravel,
buried you in lakemuck
aired you out the car window
trailed you in silken water
over the side of the boat.
Hitched around chairlegs
you tapped impatience, chafed
at the rungs till they popped
their sockets. Time came
I rode you bare again
in protest: you slapped hot
asphalt, wet sidewalks, cool tiled
floors in public buildings, your

soles grew another skin, horny
black hide I soaked off
at the end of the season.

Look at you now,
demure there, perched
on white porcelain — odd fish
half out of water, old mates — when did this
length come between us, this
body of a woman
which has already produced
out of itself other bodies?
You are still the same old
feet, preferring to go shoeless,
jumpy under tables, one of you
thumping the bed like a cat's tail
nights when sleep takes its
sweet time coming — but you are a
distance off now, beyond where I
can take you in my hands
without torsions. Feet, I
salute you here, from my own
end of the tub. I shall soak on
till the pads of your toes
wrinkle. (At my bidding
the ten of them flex towards me,
bowing.)

An Inch of Air

She wants to talk, but he
won't have it — talk — just circular
and besides, he's tired. He flicks
the lamp off, making
an end of it. And there they lie
like two cats, back to back,
in a bed too small for them.
In a moment he's under, a boy chasing
apples down a slope, some other boy
launching them down from a tree. But she,
eyes open in the dark, nerves wired,
writhes like a hooked fish on the line
of his breathing — strung in mid-air
till morning, with a quarrel to revive
over breakfast — what kind of a life. She gives
the sheets a yank — they're caught
under him — another tug
frees them, and he snores on,
uncovered. She curls up
like a spring, timed to uncoil
with the first light. And moves
an inch over, to put some token air
between her back and his.

Tides

After nine months
of strangely equal days, then ten
clocked by the press and flood
of milk, her child
eats fruit with his fingers
and scrambles after her, hands pulling her skirt.
Seasons have changed
and she hasn't noticed. One day
she woke up, and it was fall —
another, the snow was melting;
always she fell back
into the close dream where his little face
was sun and moon.
Now, like a young girl, wide-eyed
in the sudden light of outside
she feels it begin
again — like the end
of a sleep she never would have thought
possible, like the waking
of a stopped pulse ticking the world
back into being. Familiar
as an old tune, but this time felt
with a new vibration, the echo
of that huge splash upon whose ripples
she has been riding — it comes again:
the downward tug of the blood
at full moon,
amazing as the sound
of the first rain.

Nocturne

She sits up late, listening
to the wind in leaves that
may be gone tomorrow: one gust
this time of year, and up they fly,
there is no calling them back, and
it will always happen too quickly:
                              Midnight;
in the next room the child
stirs in his crib, cries out
without waking — she thinks of sleep
but sits on, unmoving; a moth
flops in the lampshade, the chairs
cast straight shadows. What
keeps her here at this hour, what —
in the plainness of things, the bare floor,
the broom in the corner, the tea stains
on the frayed tablecloth — sharpens her nerve
to the quiver of a flame-end?
She thinks: Alive.

Down the alley a dog begins barking.
The tree shakes with a knowing
the bones soon share.

At Dawn

At dawn when the lean
young men went loping
homeward from points unknown,
when their streetlamp shadows
on the blue ground
stretched long and small,
scarves
of wondrous colours
flew out behind them,
and their long hands
made fierce talk
in the air.

When the lean young men
went loping sleepward
to basement rooms, sparrows
were trying their voices'
edges against brick. The first
buses chuffed over the hill.
The lean
young men, if they craned
skyward while they fumbled
their keys in cold
barrels, saw how with
each wash of the light
above tortuous rooflines
colour drained
from the moon's face.

How oddly hung
the vestments of
the lean young men,
the outside pockets
weighted
with strange tomes!
Pens bristled in their shirts
and slid
onto the bed
when they bent to kiss
their moon-faced ladies. Other
pens, fat fountain pens
of curious vintage, slept
next to their hearts
and bled black ink
on the inside linings
of their jackets.

At two or three
in tattered paisley
dressing-gowns
the lean young men
breakfasted on sardines.
Under their eyes
the dark lines
were like war paint
no bath
drawn in a drafty john

could smooth away.
At tables
makeshift and rickety
they scratched
poems in black-bound notebooks
or transcribed
peculiar musicks of a bygone age
for the guitar.
Dusk found the
lean young men
enthroned in clouds
of bluish smoke,
poking with bristle-wires
the stems
of their gummy pipes.

The lean young men
had tongues like fish
and arms
hard as a tree
and bodies warm as furnaces
and though their kisses
tasted
like lemon cough drops
and stale tobacco,

they tossed the hair
from their eyes
with an animal grace
in those days
when they were sought
as seers
and they were loved
like gods

The umbrellas have shut

The umbrellas have shut.
They have folded
old lovers into them.
The old rainy nights
are fled, with their little
lights winking between wet
leaves, the pearled panes
under the lamps, the stairs
creaking, slick-
wet and pasted with catkins.
And the old rooms, the rooms
ornate and empty, echoing
and smelling of fresh paint —
almost
we do not remember —
and the cats on windowsills,
the hamburger smells, the guitars.

When it rains now
it is colder, we do not run
pressed close together for the nearest
café, fall's loosed leaves lie
ungathered at the curb.
The umbrellas have collapsed their domes.
They have pulled in their petals
softly dripping, have sucked
a decade into their ribs
like a sigh. Only now and then

when wind
comes charged with the old changes,
or a hat thrown on a shelf spills down
a landslide of letters
do we regret
the tall sticks
furled
in hall closets.

Erosions

Water behind a wall
makes pockets, and the years
of paint on paper over paper
peel, the layers
come away. A pipe
somewhere inside there, pipes
we hear knocking in the night,
the unseen arteries, ticking
their heat away — a pipe
cracked and bled water
down the wall. Pale amber. Paper
on paper, puckering as
water wells and fills
the pockets, pocks the wall
with peeling — this
so simple: the cause
water. Water behind a wall.

But something else erodes
our pairing, something more sinister
seeps just beneath the surface
stripping the layers where
the old glue gives. Strata
peel back, reveal
places where past repair
has failed. At last

there is no filling
the hole. We wake
to recognize the face
of slow erosion. This
so final: the old edifice,
the face of us
past patching.

Like a Blade

It has come
to be

like a blade, cutting
both ways

obsession knows how
and the spark

turning
to anger, as milk

sours; ferns uncurl
from rot, there is this,

there is this
and still

one wants it new
and raw, like green

wood, like love
when you know

it has nowhere to go
but bad.

A Valediction

Declining
frequency. Sometimes
when we laughed

it was an antler
shaken of snow.
Whole pianos opened

at a phrase. That's
gone now; the buzz,
too — but I liked

your fingernails, you know,
their curve, the full
spoons of them

September

It is the
end of summer, in fields
along the canal the smell
of white clover is strong.
The green
cigars of catalpa point down
through clusters of heart-
shaped leaf, they are
raw still, spear-like
and tough to break, the
red froth of the sumacs
wafts a fruit scent.
Finally, what have I to say
to you —walking alone here
among tall and drying weeds,
goldenrod, white sprays
of aster, the shocking blue
of chicory, that makes one see
all else in the light
of that blue? A shimmer
of insect sound is all
around me; grasshoppers
fly at my footsteps, pell-mell
into the roadside grass, I'm trying
to savour the day's gifts, each

for what it is, but thinking
how soon this ends: the clocks
of the maples already tuned
to fall —
           And there's less and less call
to imagine you, living out
your day on the other side
of the river: those streets
where pavement still absorbs
the sun's late heat all afternoon
and gives it back at evening, you're
walking there now, your shoes
don't make a sound, you've loosened
your tie and your jacket's
over your arm, above you glass
sidings catch the sunset light
and flash it down, suffusing your path
in pink, while higher still
on the hillside at the city's
heart, visible in the clefts
between buildings, show those first hints
of the colours we are supposed to find
so beautiful.

The Distance

At mid-day the chill
deserts the air, the
turning trees and the late
roses are bathed
in a warm, a dreamy
sunlight. This will last
for a little longer
if we are lucky, as
some things do last, as
even habit sometimes
glows with a warm glow.
Yet in the end the distance
is all; the colours are
contained in it, but they are
locked there, they will
never fly out like birds
or bubbles to gladden air.
Only, we can
watch them, as through glass,
in their circling. We can
name them, as we name
such stars as the city night
will show us. Is this
what we came for, then? To look
but not to touch, to leave
the prints of our fingers
singing
on a thin clear globe?

The Thread

Diminutions
of autumn. The light
makes no apology, falling
aslant the bare arms
of the trees. They have let
slide their holdings; only a
rare branch still flames
toward sundown, caught
at the right angle. The
afternoon is private, the sun
visits each window, warm
with the last warmth of October, the
screens tick in their metal
frames, mesh hazy with
last summer's dust, they ping
where a late fly, all buzz
and bluster, hurls himself
again and again. Now he has crawled
down between the screen
and outer pane, the sun
is moving on, touching the last
crescent of screen, a few
dust-motes hover there and gleam,
pearl-like, before they move
out of the light: and see,

a single thread of spider-silk,
anchored where faintest air
stirs it, gleams
and disappears, and gleams
again.

Point of Departure

The days
folding out of each other
like paper flowers. Nothing
takes your place, that's finally
understood. I kick
through leaves my stride
churns into a sound
like surf.

There are many
beautiful days, one
after another, I lose
count of them, why count them?
Strange reaches of light
across the park, a wind,
unseasonably warm, that gets
under shirts, balloons them.

It is deceptive, this wind.
I recognize you from a long way off,
turning the corner, shouldering
your empty bag. Hours
I've wasted. Weeks. How long
before snow?

The trees expose
their nests, their
perfect geometry.

Gardens on the Brink of Winter

As fast as the patch of sun
he stood in, the old man
is gone. Wind
plays the picket fence
like a comb.

To blow
on these wretched sparks —
hiss
of wind in the dried
weedstalks

beneath a window where
his widow watches,
kerchiefed
between starched
curtains:

Yellow cat
in a bare yard
skirts yellowed
grass edging the
cracked fieldstones,

darts to hollow
under porch, eyes
yellow lights waiting
for snow,
for the long nights

of snow on snow,
and the slow leak
of light from cracks
between curtains
shedding gold on snow

Interim

You're on a scaffold, I'm
down below, and you want
to talk yet — as though
talk, on such a slant, meant
anything; you, teetering there
in your high place, without
a rope, and I in a hole
where I can't see your face?
It's a joke, love. Let's wait
till there's at least a hope
of seeing eye to eye — what?
— talk about talking straight.

I'll stay here and make patterns in the gravel.
(Or, call down, and I'll hand you up your level.)

Before Snow

What a light you take
from my sky — you clouds,
closing in, breathing a
cold down — though the
sun still flames a little
at your edges — turning to
silver now, and now
a pewter sheen. You came
as winter comes, expected
but unspecific, always a
small surprise, to know it's
here now, this is it:

this is the long shadow, falling fast,
that love must rise to meet, if love's to last.

Intermezzo in a Minor Key

Cats walk the slats
of a city afternoon
in winter: and that twist
of fire-escape that skirts
your window giving
on a brick well. One imagines
how it fills up slowly
with snow — and your world
of jazz and old photographs
wavers in shifts of light
filtered down between buildings,
while smells of frying gather
on the landing, and the clumps of dust
under the peeling rads blow about a bit
in the draft from the door . . .

One thinking of you this way,
at a sharp remove, desires
no more than the evocation
of a time long past or yet to come:
"No one phoned while you were out"
or the concierge knocks to collect the rent
and the scene has its welcome shadings,
yearning held in abeyance, blurred over,
like hearing the news through the wall
on somebody else's radio.

An Early Start in Midwinter

The freeze is on. At six a scattering
of sickly lights shine pale in kitchen windows.
Thermostats are adjusted. Furnaces
blast on with a whoosh. And day
rumbles up out of cellars to the tune
of bacon spitting in a greasy pan.

Scrape your nail along the window-pane,
shave off a curl of frost. Or press your thumb
against the film of white to melt an eye
onto the fire escape. All night
pipes ticked and grumbled like sore bones.
The tap runs rust over your chapped hands.

Sweep last night's toast-crumbs off the tablecloth.
Puncture your egg-yolk with a prong of fork
so gold runs over the white. And sip
your coffee scalding hot. The radio
says you are out ahead, with time to spare.
Your clothes are waiting folded on the chair.

This is your hour to dream. The radio
says that the freeze is on, and may go on
weeks without end. You barely hear the warning.
Dreaming of orange and red, the hot-tongued flowers
that winter sunrise mimics, you go out
in the dark. And zero floats you into morning.

Zero Holding

I grow to like the bare
trees and the snow, the bones and fur
of winter. Even the greyness
of the nunneries, they are so grey,
walled all around with grey stones —
and the snow piled up on ledges
of wall and sill, those grey
planes for holding snow: this is how
it will be, months now, all so still,
sunk in itself, only the cold alive,
vibrant, like a wire — and all the
busy chimneys — their ghost-breath,
a rumour of lives warmed within,
rising, rising, and blowing away.

For the Moment

Sad is a lit window across which
no figure moves, late into evening;
sad, a watched window.

We are past the equinox.
The running sores of winter
still puddle the street.

Today there was that gentling
in the air, that brings women
to linger on their stoops;

sisters-in-law who haven't
spoken all winter, call across
to each other

and at sunset a warm wind
flings a handful of gulls
into the fire;

they revolve there, unscathed.
Let this be enough for you.
Let this and

Orion, poised whole tonight
in the small, available sky,
be enough for you.

March, Last Quarter

Liveliness only
in tiny things:
the drops of water that hang
at the tips of bare twigs

or the sparrow whose bobbings
at sapling's summit
tremor it
like a bow —

liveliness has made itself small,
has gone into tiny things
and waits there, wise, against
ice and thaw and ice
as we too wait for the air
to be kind again, taking the face
between dumb hands, breathing
love into the ear,
lifting hair.

Madrigal

There is a singular, high room, in whose lull
one has waited out love's departure.
The light falls pure there, like a note held
for voices to tune to, detached and cool,
whose true pitch lingers in the ear
like a judgment. I have avoided
this room through winter. Now, in the
early leafing, the windows are thrust
wide again, air and sun, sparrows
visit the stone sill, the flaking lintel.

I do not have to say it is good, then, our
failure of nerve: that we could not trust
love in each other. At least I do not have
to say that it was good, or just as well.

Yours

May deepens its greens, widens the
ends of days, and I see you
far from me, moving in the cool
of evening, the precious light.
How bright the hours have grown
since you turned away. Now your
windows are full of sky and
leaves only, I shade my eyes
to no avail, there is nothing to see
or say. But once or twice a day
I look up, startled by a fluid
movement of leaves, I gaze at those
mirrors behind which you live
your life that is your life.

Little Prelude

Triggered by wind, the twinned
and single wings copter
off maples. Wind
rasps their dry webbing
against pavement, where children,
playing, alone, scoop
handfuls to husk
down to the sappy bean.

Oh summer's big quilted winds
bolstering scent!   the chestnut's
gleaming pyramids, catalpa
shaking its frilly bells down
to grass. Green
barely remembered, under
cloud cover, green lit
from within, June green, how it

jumps our eyes, moments
before rain, when the length
of the emptying street, heavy
windows gibber shut
in their wooden frames.

On My Son's Birthday

Already the beans have begun their wild climb,
twining tough runners round and round each string
we anchored to the porch above our own.
Only a month ago, you helped me press
the seeds we popped from dry brown pods last fall
into the holes you poked with your small fingers.

Today you wake me, holding up five fingers
to mark your years, triumphant, as you climb
beside me into bed, but not to fall
asleep again. Later you know we'll string
balloons, wrap favours. Eager, your cold feet press
for warmth, toes curled tight, against my own.

This is our day, this day you call your own.
Five years ago today, I counted fingers,
touched perfect limbs, and felt your small mouth press
against my nipple. After our breathless climb
we lay together, linked by a tough string
cut cleanly to allow your perfect fall.

First-fruit; conceived, not like our beans, in fall,
popped from the pod in summer. This has its own
logic, I think; I touch it like a string
and feel it resonate beneath my fingers.
The months are like the scale's twelve tones we climb
yearly, as toward this fundament they press.

Born at the solstice. Born when light's clean press
toward summer scales its height and points to fall,
but when the vines have just been begun their climb
into the light to rhythms of their own
with leaves uncurling like a baby's fingers.
This is the day the arrow left the string.

Lying beside me now, taut as that string
with all the day's solemnity, you press
your hand against my hand to measure fingers,
show me scraped knuckles from a recent fall,
tell me you'd like a scooter of your own.
Outside, the sun begins its perfect climb.

My sprout, my vine, my own, God guard your climb
and string you toward your flowering. As my years press
toward fall, I count my blessings on your fingers.

Meridian

Your enormous suns dwarfing narrow houses
holding their brave chimneys slightly awry,
your suns sticking their spokes out like ships' wheels,
not quartered in a corner of the sky
but veering toward center, looming over figures
to swallow or protect them? how can I know –

your suns have made a liar of me. I know
I said I'd not make poems about crude houses
children draw, kids' paintings. Well, it figures.
Much that I balanced on has gone awry
in the new light of you: the very sky,
it seemed at times, turned round us – wheels within wheels.

Like a lone walker in noon heat, who wheels,
sudden, on no-one (what is this fear we know,
this sense of being followed?) under a sky
whose sun beats like a pulse on the mute houses
and something in the landscape seems awry,
unreal, a postcard scene with brittle figures;

or like a tiny skater turning figures
on some immense field, balanced on blades or wheels –
I watch you brave a world that turns awry
all armour I can give you, all that I know
of fancy footwork; though your body houses
all I could call my faith beneath the sky.

So your huge hovering suns, that fill the sky,
are hope I hold against the damning figures
that would lift off the roofs of our brave houses,
blow us to kingdom come like catherine wheels.
The way you draw a sun tells me you know
the need to know a source need bent awry.

Soon you will learn its power to twist awry
all that its brightness touches. Soon your sky
must darken with the weight of what men know,
the horror they can wrest from balanced figures.
Draw your great suns, your primal colour-wheels,
with rays like arms that reach out to the houses.

Draw your brave suns, your captains'-wheels. And know
that what's awry lies only in the figures.
Oh steer our houses by a safer sky!

Black Walnut

We found those funny green balls in the grass,
perfumy as unripe oranges, but hard,
and bleeding rank iodine when cut open,
leaving their stain deep in the palms' creases.
The stone inside was hard to hack away
from the raw flesh of the stubborn fruit.

Now, heading into winter, one fruit
of the several we picked up that day in the grass
sits on the sill, where I put it away
to see if it would ripen. Blackish, rock hard
though light as pumice, it has dried in ridged creases.
It would take a hammer to break this open.

But who would ever think of breaking it open?
It seems an artifact now, not a fruit.
Its history is sealed into these creases
as ice preserves the lay of the tangled grass.
I have no use for this thing; why is it hard
to decide the time has come to throw it away?

Maybe because the scent has not gone away,
and the faint spice of it has power to open
thought-ways to other things grown soft or hard
with age or their own failure to yield fruit
(though they persist, unkillable as the grass
that, flattened, springs back up from its own creases.)

I think how ice moves over the earth, and creases
the face of it, or grinds the edges away,
leaving a smooth bed for the blanketing grass.
I think how, in the rock, deep fissures open
and endure to become valleys, lush with fruit —
and then, how rotting trees have turned stone hard.

And I think of the passion to preserve, the hard
clear light that loves to register the creases
in a face, or a cloth with an arrangement of fruit:
as if recording these could hold away
the shadow of that chasm we know must open
soon at our feet, in the supple familiar grass.

Hard as its nut, this mummy of a fruit
creases the brow. The mind drifts far away,
open to every current in the grass.

The Aging Woman with Braids

And of the balancing acts
of squirrels, of cats, I say
they do recover themselves;

And of the man who walked
a crooked mile, I say
he will remember it;

And of the wet letter, peeled
from rainy pavement, I say
best not read that . . .

Look! how Love is spawned
in the air, between the white hands
of Pierrot; how it floats there, thin and
inviolate, a bubble, reflecting
the tenderness of his smile —

    I am taking five umbrella steps
    in my Chinese cloth shoes.
    Mother, may I?

Water on the Chair

Things we want
in the dark —
because —

the lop-eared lamb
wedged between wall
and frame, him,

smelling of mildew
and old pee —
called for

a hundred times
without emphasis,
with a blind

insistence, need
to have him
dragged up

dusty and begrudged
from that place
we can't see —

Things we call for
in the dark,
uncalled-for —

the full glass
near to hand
sipped from   once only

along whose sides
by morning
small pearls have formed — .

Here on Earth

The child is learning the laws of perspective;
with his thumb, he can cover his father's face,
with his palm, he blots whole buildings.
At the right distance, the keyhole — imagine it —
can contain the landlady, fat as she is;
so it would not surprise him if the odd camel
slipped through the eye of a needle.

Heaven is full of rich men,
but the poor, the poor,
(subject to the laws
of perspective, and
other laws) — the poor
are here on earth
for a long time.

In Winter Rooms

In winter rooms, the sad grey light settles on breakfast remains. On the knife that rests against the saucer, and on the crumbs in the glass dish. On the crumbs in the butter. And the piece of burnt toast with two bites out of it, left to get cold on the tablecloth.

It is the same light, whether morning or afternoon. It picks out the new cracks in the plaster, the streaks on the ceiling; it catches the tremble of a long feather of soot which hangs by an invisible hair from a joint in the chimney-pipe. The sad grey light comes leaking through dirty panes; it circles the room like a ghost and does not chase the shadows. Only the round belly of the brown teapot, glazed and shining, catches a gleam of it and flashes it back like a drop of water.

Outside, snow piles on the balcony rail and on the sill. A rag flaps in the balcony tree; it has been flapping there for a hundred days. Torn plastic billows out from the shed windows. Sometimes there are sparrows; they don't sing though. The leaves of the house-plants dry and curl up; now and then one falls off and crumbles into dust. Wind comes down the chimney and blows the smell of oilsoot into the house.

In a corner of the kitchen, the old woman rocks and rocks in the rocking-chair. The young woman is making bread, pounding the dough on a wooden board. A dust of flour is on the air. She pounds and thumps the dough until her strong knuckles ache, and then she oils a bowl in which to let it rise.

The child plays on the floor. She has begged a piece of dough for her own, and has rolled it between her palms until it is grey and without resilience. Now its creases persist; it will no longer roll back into smoothness. The child tires of it; she asks to take down the green vase from the shelf, the vase with the chipped rim. She empties it of its contents: stray buttons, pennies, hairpins, a single earring, pencil-stubs, and keys that don't belong to anything. These she picks up one by one and examines intently, dropping some back into the vase and making a little pile of others beside her right knee.

The rockers wear away the pattern on the linoleum.
The child discovers her face in a spoon, upside down.
The young woman punches the dough down and forms it into loaves.

The rockers fret and fret against the floor; they wear the pattern off the linoleum.
The teapot like a dark bubble reflects the sad grey square of window.
The child bites into an orange and peels it. The essence

stings the air. She offers a wedge to the young woman, who takes it and eats. She offers a wedge to the old woman, who does the same.

On the shelf above the stove, the loaves rise.

Study in Latex Semi-Gloss

There is nothing new. Does that matter? Somewhere a woman is painting her rooms. She has tied up her hair and covered it with a tattered diaper. Alone, in a flat lit by bare bulbs, she moves from room to room, her sandals sticking to the spread pages of old Gazettes pooled with paint spills. She is looking for something, for a screwdriver with a yellow handle, with which she now pries off the lid of the last can of paint; she is stirring the paint with a wooden stick, stirring it longer than necessary, as if it were batter. Now she pours creamy fold upon fold into the crusted tray. The telephone shrills in another room; it is you, but she won't get there in time to answer. If she did, what could you say that would apply here?

Late into the night bare windows frame her, bending and stretching, wielding the roller on its broomstick. Paint streaks her bare arms and legs; some hairs have escaped the cloth about her head to fall in her eyes, and she pushes them aside with the clean back of her hand. In the alley behind the flat, cats couple with strangled yells. Soon she will shut herself in the tiny bath, blinking at the dazzle which dulls the fixtures to the colour of stained teeth; she will tack a torn towel over the window and drop her clothes — the loose jersey with the sleeves cut off, the frayed corduroy shorts, stiff with spatters of paint, at whose edges bunches of dark thread dangle. The underpants, damp and musky with sweat, will fall limp to her ankles. She will squat in the narrow tub, scrubbing at her skin with washcloth, solvent, fingernails, and after, with the cracked remnant of a bar of green soap which she tries in vain to work into a lather. Rinsing with splashed water, she'll pause and hug her knees, hug in the sag of her tired breasts, then stand, stretch, pat dry with the clean side of a damp towel. On the toilet she'll bend to examine a broken toenail and remain bent, dreaming, staring at the yellowed tiles.

You will have been asleep an hour, by the time she kills the lights and slips naked into a sleeping-bag spread across a bare mattress on the bare floor. The smell of the bag is the smell of woodsmoke and pine, faint, mixed with old sweat. Perhaps it's the smell that makes her smile a little as she feels herself sucked down into the whirlpool of sleep. Somewhere across blocks and blocks of tenements, her children, half-grown, long-limbed, sprawling on foam mats in their father's studio apartment, will stir as a lone car guns its engine in the empty street. She dreams, if she dreams at all, of holes in the plaster, of places where the baseboard is missing, of the bulging and cracking of imperfect surfaces. Dreams the geography of a wall.

There is nothing new. Even what could bloom between you, if you let it, if she let it, goes on as the paint goes on, over old seams, old sutures. Weathers as the paint will weather, flaking along old stress lines. This matters. Think, before you dial again. What have you to do with those children, blinking sleep from their eyes, breakfasting with their father in a booth of the local diner; where will you be when daylight, like cold water, shocks her awake to pull on yesterday's clothes and squat in the kitchen doorway with her mug of instant coffee? Where, when her clear eyes, steady in their purpose, scan the new surface to discover her painter's holidays?

Anyone Skating on that Middle Ground

Like a child, sights set elsewhere, you throw away what's offered you. What you asked for, without thinking Do I want this? Have I the right? and what you look at now as though it came from another planet.

We were waiting for a break in the weather. We were waiting for the light to change. We were waiting for the performance to begin, and then we were waiting for it to end. We were waiting from someone to notice that we were waiting. In no hurry at all, we waited for them to bring us the bill.

Time and it seems and it seems. Time seems. And time and time. And seems time passing passing. Seems passing seems the time and the time not passing. Pass and it seems past seeming. Pass. And pass.

Over your shoulder I see them pass the window. Man with an arm around a girl, girl crying. Night glare on her wet cheek, the wet street neon-stained. She has broken away from him and run ahead; he has called after her, in tones of disbelief, and it has only made her quicken her step; he stops in the middle of the sidewalk and calls her again, more sharply, but she keeps on walking. At last in a few running strides he overtakes her and she concedes to the hand on her shoulder by slowing her pace a little but not by ceasing to cry; I see her shake her head vigorously once, twice; she has nothing to say to him. And so they walk along together, too swiftly, seeing nothing around them, wrapped in the distance of their moment.

Distance is a word that you like, another is suggestion, and you are fond also of contour and surface. Given the chance, you will qualify even that. Am I right? You guess that you don't want to discuss it. These cool spring days, you are answering your own question at every turn, but it seems you don't listen to yourself. When the boiling point is reached, pressure builds up and steam is forced out through a tiny hole in the lid. This is why the kettle sings.

We were waiting for a change in the weather. We thought that this, after all, was what it hinged on; that the old succession of small miracles, ice breaking, blades pushing up, warm rainy night smells, would be enough to start the movement again. That was what we thought we wanted: to be moved, to begin to move again. For the little things to do it to us, as they used to in the days when God loved us.

She thinks that she is beginning to get the message. He supposes that it's not his affair. When he wakes up, he can tell by a quality of the quiet in the house that she has already left for work. The tidiness of the kitchen is chastening. The coffee is still warm. The flowers are in the window, and the window's open.

Nature Walk

In the long grass of a country graveyard, my children find a bird's-egg, intact, china blue, so perfectly small they gasp to see it. How did it fall without breaking?

Another year they find a dead cicada in a weed-choked city yard; their father preserves it in an empty spice-bottle. Wings like lace kites; faint smell of cardamom.

In his drawer, rummaging for matches, I come across a curious brown knobbled thing, hard as a pebble but wrinkled, I take it for peyote and quiz him, a bit surprised. He laughs, it is the stump, he says, of our son's umbilical cord, he saved it when it fell off.

On the mountain these Sundays, we pick seed-pods of milkweed, we break open the spiky husks of horse-chestnut to extract the gleaming kernels, we gather berries of mountain-ash, pieces of bark and leaves we don't recognize. We fill our pockets with them. But my daughter finds a thorn-bush with thorns as long as her thumb, thin black daggers, razor-straight. She breaks off a twig of these, who will carry it for her so she doesn't hurt herself? It is this above all she wants to bring home.

Detour

An unexpected turn, and the bus leaves you by a corner you've not seen before — just a bit of city, neat flats above small store fronts, small front yards, here by the corner post a bushel basket planted with zinnias, there a locust tree, blowing against brick, the leaves untidy with autumn. Rain in the air. At your back a corner grocer's; with each swing of the door, whiffs of ripe fruit, of scented soap and onions. Look, across the street an old barber-shop, the striped pole revolving, and the barber moody, hands in pockets, gazing out through plate glass — motionless as the empty chairs behind him.

Sparrows, loud in a hedge. The leaves showing their undersides. You're not sure what street you're on, but you have your transfer, and what else is needed? This is the day's sole surprise, to find yourself for a short spell in this spot you'll likely not see again, though you pass close to it daily. A place of no importance in the frame of what you call your life. You hope the bus will come before the rain does, you like the look of the lights now, in the shop windows. That's as far as you want to think it, holding your ground here for the time required, taking at face value this place that counts for today only. The place where you count to ten and take the blindfold off. Where you stand and wait, on faith, for your next connection.

Suckers for Truth

How much longer do you suppose
we can get away with it, edging
a little closer to the fire, sitting up
long past midnight, stubborn holdouts
in the unseasonable cold? The effects
of too much wine, of wine at the wrong time
have begun to take their toll, dredging up moments
that had gone unnoticed, but return now
to trouble us, like a funny noise
in the engine, that we register gradually
but manage to avoid talking about for miles

The landscape falls away
on either side of us, some of the trees
already turning, far ahead a darkening
as yet more felt than seen, seeming to indicate
we're heading into a storm front
and we don't care, do we, switching the radio
to another station, watching the signs
for a roadside diner, somewhere to unzip
and grab a sandwich, coffees to take out,
while we congratulate ourselves
for making good time

It's not as though we aren't aware
of the pitfalls, but that we know
procrastination is our best defence,
so far we have not committed ourselves

and it shows, there's that comfortable rubble
on the seats and floor we'd have to clear away
to get down to business, oddly festive
and a bit risqué, till now it has seemed
easiest to tack strips of old carpeting
over the cracks, when the thing falls apart
we're hoping it will do it all at once

A camp stool, a tin pot, and an old
umbrella, stage props for a stay
against confusion, we find ways
to laugh at the rain, and in it,
and to accommodate our guests, so much
depends on the things glimpsed
in the rear-view mirror, wheelbarrows
and such, it seems that with luck
a kind of courtship happens between the lines
and it's this we're after: without the risk
what would be possible?

A Meditation Between Claims

You want to close your hand
on something perfect, you want to say
Aha. Everything moves towards this,
or seems to move, you measure it
in the inches you must let down
on the children's overalls,
tearing the pages off the wall
each month; a friend phones
with news that another friend
has taken Tibetan vows, meanwhile the
kitchen is filling up with the smell
of burnt rice, you remind yourself
to buy postage stamps tomorrow

The mover
and the thing moved, are they two
or one; if two, is the thing moved
within or without, questions
you do not often bother yourself with
though you should; the corner store
is closed for the high holy days,
and though the air has a smell
not far from snow, your reluctance
to strip the garden is understandable

Laundry is piling up
in the back room, Mondays and Thursdays
the trash must be carried out

or it accumulates, each day
things get moved about and
put back in their places
and you accept this, the shape
that it gives a life, though the need
to make room supercedes other needs

If, bidding your guest goodbye,
you stand too long at the open door,
house-heat escapes, and the oil bill
will be higher next month, the toll
continues, wrapping the green tomatoes
in news of the latest assassination.
The mover
and the thing moved, it all
comes down to this: one wants
to sit in the sun like a stone,
one wants to move the stone; which
is better

Refilling the Spirit Lamp

For awhile desire is fuel.
And the distance gained
always is illusory.
There's a luminescence young
leaves can't hold very long
in their greening, or the air
in early spring, when it is cool
and frangible, that is
something like what we thought
had been promised:

how a cup, a lamp, a chair
are so much more than that,
or the scarf you left behind, a
handful of loose change on the bureau.
Someone saw a common thread there
and named it, but he didn't know
how close a brush it had been.

What burns now
is something else, something we hope
could be more dependable, riding out
a run of bad weather, how these
evenings find us back in our rooms
over paper, our lamps tuned low,
and an ear for the finest of nuances
bent to that tuning.

The Search

for David and Hilari

The search begins again, just
when you thought you'd arrived, or
anyway ceased to stumble, grown
content with randomness, with wandering
as an end in itself. You like the
woods, even at night, the fields
mornings or afternoons, you've beaten a
path in the long grass from the back door
to your spot overlooking the valley.
Little enough you care if your foot slips
into the odd bog, take that as a cue
to stretch out in clover, chewing
on a grass-blade while your socks
dry out in the sun. What else
could you say you wanted? Even so
you feel it come on, sometimes, like the
mournful magic of those augmented
triads the frogs raise, their long, slow
trills bubbling up in the moonlight.

It has never helped to think you knew
what you were looking for, and now
you know you don't: that maybe when all's said
it isn't you who look, but someone
or something out there, in the watchful
dark, that has followed you to this pass
and waits only for you to walk
unwitting into its arms. Night itself

is full of surprises, a stray firefly
winks in the windbent upper branches
of the pine grove, clouds
cocoon the moon
and you stand still, thinking it's
right beside you — there — or there —
though your hands close only
on air, and once again the frogs sing
something you've never heard before.

Sounding an Old Chord
in October

The streetlamp directly opposite
is out, an unaccustomed dark
pools this side of the street.
In the garden the dried bean-pods
rasp on their woody vines,
leave nothing to look forward to
but snow. Still, expectation
stirs, a dog with ears cocked
for familiar footsteps, lights
in strange windows are taking on
a peculiar intimacy
                        It's the old story,
the thing we'd almost forgotten, last year's
chestnut, bone-smooth to cold fingers
fishing a linty pocket for a fare
(though the rates have gone up again
since the coat was hung away, and any
loose change is purely fortuitous)

A pebble
ricochets off the bus-stop
with the kind of ping metal only makes
when cold, like the twang
of a piano-string that slips
in the dead of night
                        so expecting
the unexpected becomes a way of saying
yes again, this is the thing
we refuse to go on without,

the delicate engineering of a life
to allow for a coincidence of paths,
take it from there

For no other reason
we stare at a little piece of street
between buildings, as if we could will
the arrival of someone unlikely to pass there,
spontaneous, nonchalant
with neither wine nor flowers,
just a dark figure jaunting along
in no sort of hurry
and visible only for seconds
between parked cars.

Scratch

The tinder words, where are they,
the ones that
jump-start the heart —

    like mirrors at the bends
    of tunnels, that withhold
    your face, but give you
    what is to come;

    like the voice at the end
    of the tunnel, that says
    'Terminus,' almost
    tenderly —

Little twigs that snap
like gunshot as they
consume themselves, little
dry twigs,

little sparks, little pops, little bursts
at the smoky heart of where it
begins again, o,

tender and sunny love! what, are you gone
so far away?

Come home to me now, my

brightness. Make a small glow.
Make it to move
the heart, that has sat down
in the road

and waits for something
to turn it over . . .

      The roomy heart,
      willing to be surprised.

The Cyclist Recovers
his Cadence

i

When the front wheel
glances off something hard
you are thrown over
the handlebars and slap
pavement with a crunch
of bone. In that instant
a hole opens under you
and it goes clear down
to the howling center.
You wake there. It is awhile
before you become aware
of an odd jazz playing
and longer still before your feet
begin to move to it.

Nothing can be the same
from here. The smells
that blow in open windows
of an evening: honeysuckle
and fried potatoes, a mix
sure to confuse   even your childhood
has an unfamiliar patina
when you lie awake
remembering it. Summer
is upon you: heat, the sticky
surfaces of things. You long
strangely for thunder, but when it comes

it's not the ticket.
The old box has cracks in it.
The old box
               The crank
on the ice cream bucket
slips a gear. Children
gather, they jump like flies
around a lamp, bouncing
off each other. One, the biggest,
thwacks the ice in a burlap sack
against the concrete step.
Your bad arms gives out
as the mixture stiffens.
Switch to the left. The crew
runs home for spoons.

Later, cutting the grass
to work off steam, coming out
in the dark to dust the beets
with rotenone, unkinking
the garden hose, nothing
means what you thought it did,
your mother's letter invoking God
notwithstanding, you draw a blank
in the higher uncertainties.
Enough if in the after-dinner hours
neighbours gather on the stoops
till long past dark, enough

that your son dances barefoot
on the pavement, blowing
harmonica tunes to the night street.

ii

Summer
sprints fallward, but all else
is sluggish, still. The clothes
on the line hang damp for days.
Noon vibrates
like sheet metal
Cicadas drill
        Fruit-flies
cluster to kiss the broken skins
of blue plums rotting on the window-sill.

The body's knit itself.
You celebrate your thirtieth
on the muggiest day of summer.
Somewhere a bicycle-wheel
spins on, up-ended,
and though you know the trick
that's kept it going, its oilsmooth
tickticktick still calibrates
the space between sleep and waking.
The spokes flash in the sun
and seem
to reverse direction. When it stops —

iii

becomes-still.
One piano tone struck in an empty room.
Pain's stab
ebbing. The candle
drowning in its own wax.

Spun to nothing.
No end, but
continuum.
Beginnings flow out of this.

Soft pedalling the *da capo*,
the soul's progress
diminuendo.

iv

At the bottom of the key
fullness hangs
on a fingertip. See,
a moon-sliver; the blanched
rim of the nail.
Blood presses
against it. At rest

like this, sunk
in a tuned stillness
the hand becomes
capable of motion.

You are working your way back
towards a more placid grammar.
Your son points at the moon
and laughs. You carry him to bed.

If the little fox gets his tail in the water,
what could further?

                    v

Delicately between her teeth
your grandmother cracks
blanched almonds into
their clean, separate halves.
Sunset from a folding chair.
Your mother on the screened porch
calls a warning. A clear
soprano
                    You are stepping over
the wire fence, you are putting
one foot down
into the fields. Ping!
a grasshopper flies up

like a sprung paper-clip.
Ping   Ping   A tawny sea
closes back over them. One
step more, and a knot
in the grass unfoots you,
flings you on your face
in prickles. You cry
and they run to lift you back
into the garden. A bird
pipes in the thicket. Soon
they will carry you to bed.

The moon comes out
like a chip of blanched almond.

vi

Take it again from the beginning,
run the reel backward
to the point of collision,
repeat the vault
in slow motion.
There was your chance,
there is what
you must all along have been
waiting for, it will
happen again, you have been
primed. While the wheel spins

the spokes wink out their music.
Take your boy's hands
and dance. Complete
these revolutions
till the neat
rebuff, the unseating,
the somersault into
another country.

Walking a Dog in the Rain

— If the shoe fits, wear it.

These lessons in patience
weren't asked for. Among
so much else, I'm learning
to recognize them for the gift
they probably are. Like
the rest of it: the varied shades
of brick darkened by rain, odours
of back sheds, mildewed
and dark with promise, bent
objects reaching odd lengths out
from heaps of rotting board
                              It's true
that I've wanted more, again, balanced
against so much I thought I'd
given up on, leaning
on the porch rail, evenings, dreaming my
scrap of yard — what
will grow here? what can grow?
the question like a shy palm
turned up to catch the rain, is this
how it begins, will it be
different this time?

The waiting
obliterates itself, has come to be
a formal exercise, diminishing
in tension, almost a dance,
though months elapse

between gestures and it doesn't matter
in the way that it used to

I like a white wall,
a good lamp, shadows
of leaves, I can live with these
a long time, even
without music, the right pictures
will show up, one at a time, when you're
not looking for them, all the
small touches you've come to expect
are best done without at first,
giving you time
to grow neutral, pure, to shed
the crust of what was

You play back the tape
of nothing happening in your house
and it's nice, it's
just like being there:
                      moments
that can still make me smile

Tracing
and retracing of steps, the paths
now familiar, every pause,
every turn, alleys, vacant lots,
the brickpiles and back fences

with gaps one can navigate, the lamp posts
one lingers under at predictable hours

And again the urge to say
come home now, come in
out of the rain, this is the
hardest lesson, the final one, not
to say it, leave the way clear
for you to recognize what's yours
and claim it
                    a gentle city, generous
in its leaves, the porch lights
burn late there, the double doors
stand open, even now, letting in
fragrance of linden, flowers
litter the stoop where rain drips
from the eaves, wind blows through the
empty rooms, finally
this will always
be enough

To Fill a Life

To fill a life as fitful sky fills windows, or a painter, canvas, to fill it willfully, to make large movements within a frame, I think is to be desired — the frame, too, not to contain, but to provoke such movement. No mirror will show you the lines worry pushes your face into, for in the looking, curiosity makes other lines. I want to move far enough away to see you whole, as a child will in a loop that he makes of finger and thumb. *Look how small I can make you, Mummy.*

So the unmade beds of children. So the hats, scarves, mitts, thrown pell-mell over the radiator, so the smell of damp wool filling the hall as the heat rises. On the counter, the jagged shells of breakfast eggs, a crust of stuck whites like brown lace in the cast iron skillet still warm on the burner. So the towels on the bathroom floor, the steamed mirror, stray hairs in the tub and a blue worm of dried toothpaste on the edge of the sink. The tap dripping, humid air smelling of shampoo. The face of a life in motion. The pegs on the rack by the door, on which are slung umbrellas, shawls, soft bags of cloth and leather, the straps wound round each other.

To delight in the weathered, more than in polished planes, to prefer the visible repair to the thing re-done, I think is to respect tenancy, its wear and tear, its fixed term. For each grey hair he pulls from her head, she gives her youngest son a penny, until there are so many, he makes a bankrupt of her, no more, she throws up her hands, laughing. Decades later, when she sells the old house, he comes at night and removes from its hinges the door to the back shed, into whose reluctant grain he and his brothers gouged their names and a date, in boyhood. He puts it on his car, he drives it home and stores it under his stairs. Three names on an unhinged door, the first, of a man dead these twenty-two years. All winter, snow blows into the old shed.

To fill a life. To fill one's own shoes, and walk in them till the plies of the soles begin to separate, till the heels are rubbed away, till the toes turn up and the lettering inside has all flaked off. As fitful sky. To go with the drift of things, shifts of the light and weather. Snow blows into the tracks my skis made this morning: erase all that. I am walking on the face of winter. It's like magic, it's like walking on water, it *is* walking on water. Are you listening? I know a man who photographs the bumps on faces, the tiny lines, who celebrates them with his sharpest focus. I know a man who broke his hammer trying to open a window. Each winter new cracks open in the chimney wall, air currents trace fresh strata of soot across the ceiling.

A pulling against the grain. Amoebas of light in the undulation of gauze curtains, the cross and mesh of lines. Water's resistance as the oars reverse direction. Walking upwind. Syncopation, in music, or certain kinds of dissonance. Cloth cut on the bias, hair combed up from the nape. Velvet, rubbed the wrong way with a finger. Or finger and thumb, cleansed to an edge, testing each other's raised grain. Feeling the lines that frame us, whorl and loop, for life, beyond confusion.

I want to move far enough away to see you whole, I want a lens to contain you, even upside down, as a handful of cast type contains its own impression. As winter contains spring, or the residue of snow, the shape of those things it melted around. The broken tricycle, the rusted spade. It is spring, the season for construction; no backward look in the way that old house is gutted for renovation. I watch from across the street, chunks of my life knocked out like bad teeth, the plaster-dust drifting down like a chalky pall over the gardens. Erase all that. Are you listening?

The face of a life in motion. The sound of pianos out of open windows; radios playing to empty kitchens. On the cold sidewalk, a ring of footsteps: that sound nearly forgotten. Clotheslines shrilling on rusty pulleys; the squeak of baby-carriage wheels. Or close your eyes and it's June, pages torn from a child's copy-book are blowing down the street. In the park, by the stone pond, a line of figures in loose clothing practice Tai Chi, their movements sweeping, rhythmical, echoing each other like the arches of the pavillion behind them, reflected in the water. It's early morning. The movements are large, are generous, they flow, and the clothing too as it fills with wind, flapping against the bodies held there in marvelous postures against the light.

A Note on the Selection

The selection of poems from earlier books is my own, as is the sequence. I first considered a chronological sequence, grouping the poems book by book, but in the end it seemed more interesting to mix them, allowing "sound and sense" to determine an order.

In the resulting sequence, some elements of chronology remain: most of the poems written prior to 1980 are towards the beginning. The opening five poems are the only ones taken from my first book, *Shadowplay*. Since these are very early poems, I found it hard to place them among the rest.

A bibliography of individual poems is included on page 141.

Acknowledgements

Various poems from *The Touchstone* appeared first in the following publications:

Prism International, The Antigonish Review, Queen's Quarterly, Versus, University of Windsor Review, The Malahat Review, The Canadian Forum, Poetry Canada Review, West Coast Review, Rubicon, ellipse, Prairie Fire, Matrix, *Aurora 1980* (Doubleday), *Cross/cut* (Véhicule), *The Inner Ear* and *Full Moon* (Quadrant), *Canadian Poetry Now* (Anansi), *The New Canadian Poets* (McClelland and Stewart), *15 Canadian Poets × 2* and *Poetry by Canadian Women* (Oxford), *The Other Language* (The Muses Company).

"On My Son's Birthday," "Meridian," and "Black Walnut" were first published as *Three Sestinas* in February 1984 in an edition of 130 copies, by Villeneuve Publications.

Bibliography of Selected Poems

From *Shadowplay* (Fiddlehead Poetry Books, University of New Brunswick, Fredericton, 1978):
  Sinkers, Broom at Twilight, October/Sutton, I think of your hands, He hears her on the stairs

From *The Space Between Sleep and Waking* (Villeneuve Publications, Montreal, 1981):
  Fugue, Maintenance, Cat's Cradle, End to End, An Inch of Air, Tides, Nocturne, At Dawn, Erosions, An Early Start in Midwinter, In Winter Rooms, The Cyclist Recovers his Cadence

From *Anyone Skating on that Middle Ground* (Vehicule Press, Montreal, 1984):
  Paperweight, Pardon Me, The umbrellas have shut, Like a Blade, A Valediction, Gardens on the Brink of Winter, Intermezzo in a Minor Key, Little Prelude, On My Son's Birthday, Meridian, Black Walnut, Water on the Chair, Study in Latex Semi-Gloss, Anyone Skating on that Middle Ground, Suckers for Truth, A Meditation Between Claims, Refilling the Spirit Lamp, The Search, Sounding an Old Chord in October

From *Becoming Light* (Cormorant Books, Dunvegan, Ontario, 1987):
  Woman on a Bus, September, The Distance, The Thread, Point of Departure, Interim, Before Snow, Zero Holding, For the Moment, March, Last Quarter, Madrigal, Yours, The Aging Woman with Braids, Here on Earth, Nature Walk, Detour, Scratch, Walking a Dog in the Rain, To Fill a Life

Printed in Canada